# Anna Banana
## and the
# Chocolate Explosion!

By Dominique Roques
Illustrated by Alexis Dormal

**:01**

**First Second**
New York

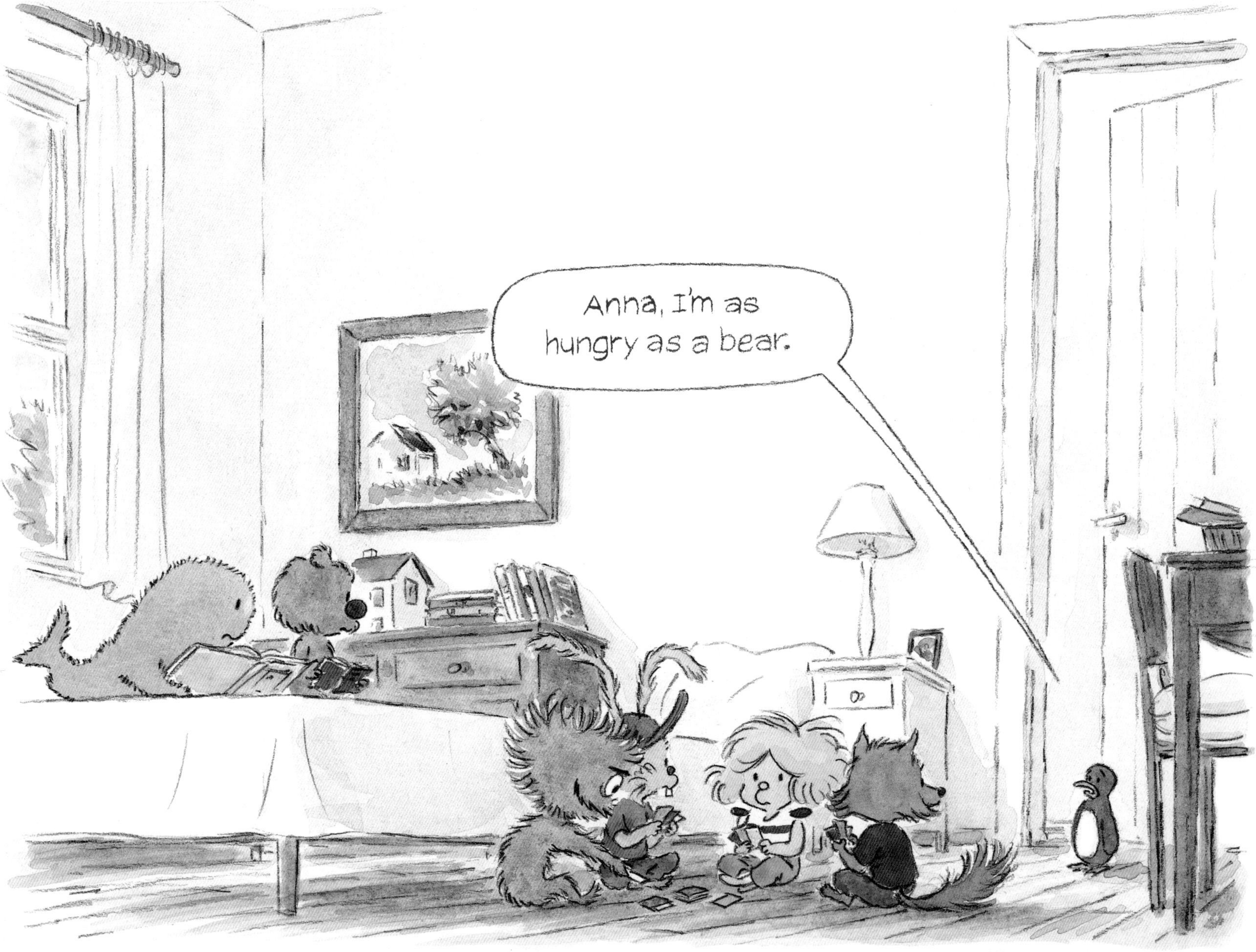
Anna, I'm as hungry as a bear.

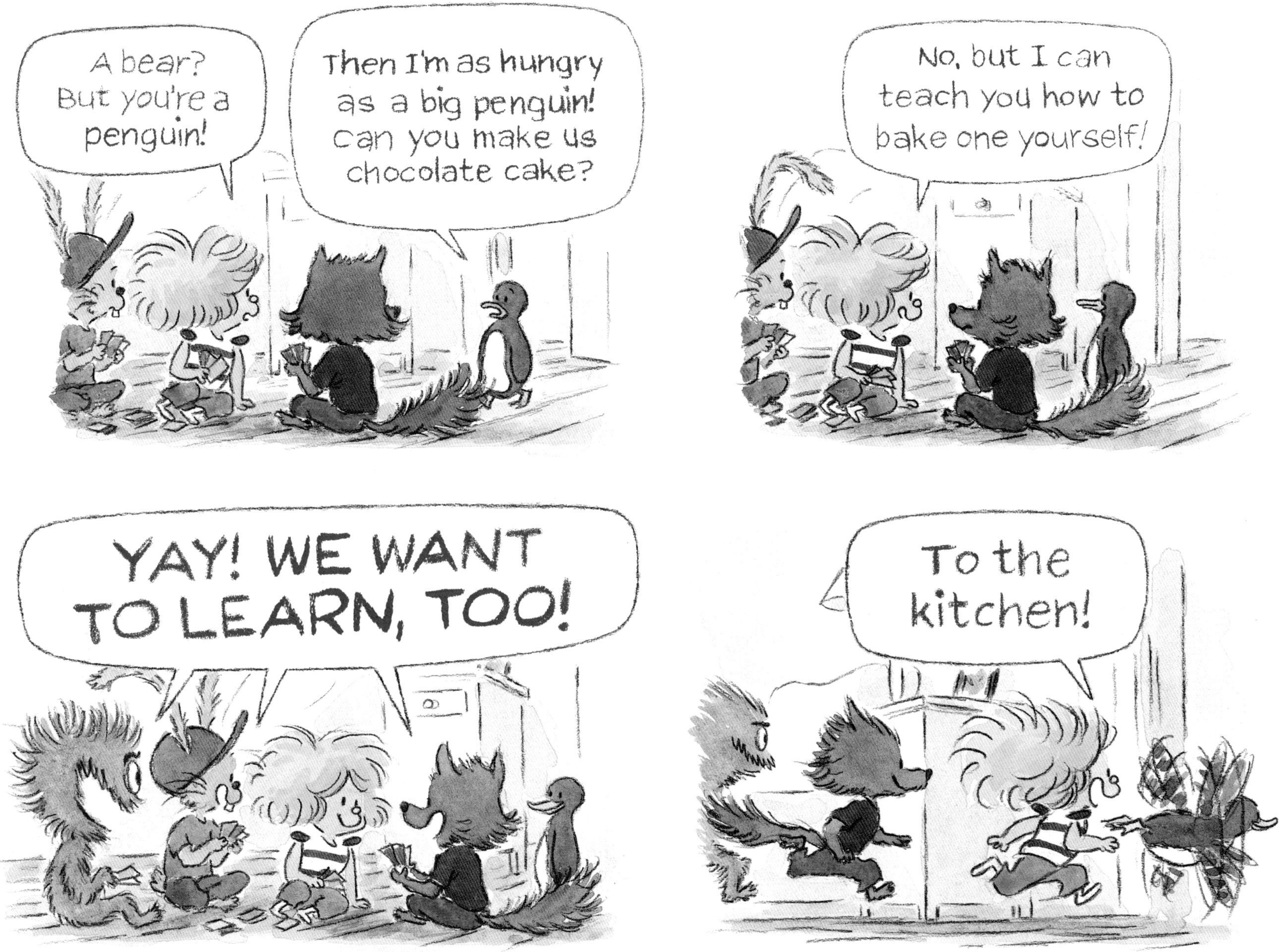
A bear? But you're a penguin!
Then I'm as hungry as a big penguin! Can you make us chocolate cake?
No, but I can teach you how to bake one yourself!
YAY! WE WANT TO LEARN, TOO!
To the kitchen!

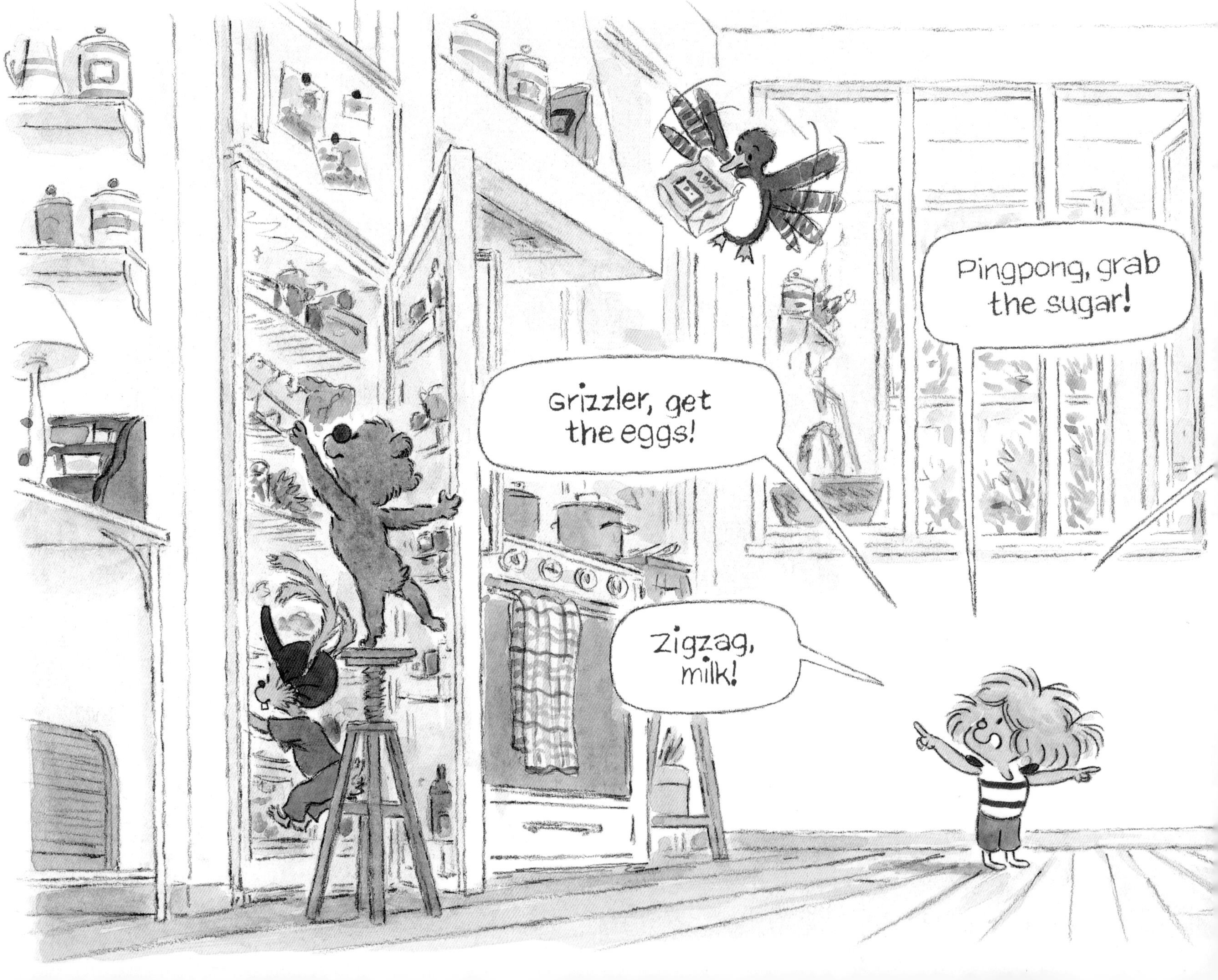
Pingpong, grab the sugar!
Grizzler, get the eggs!
Zigzag, milk!

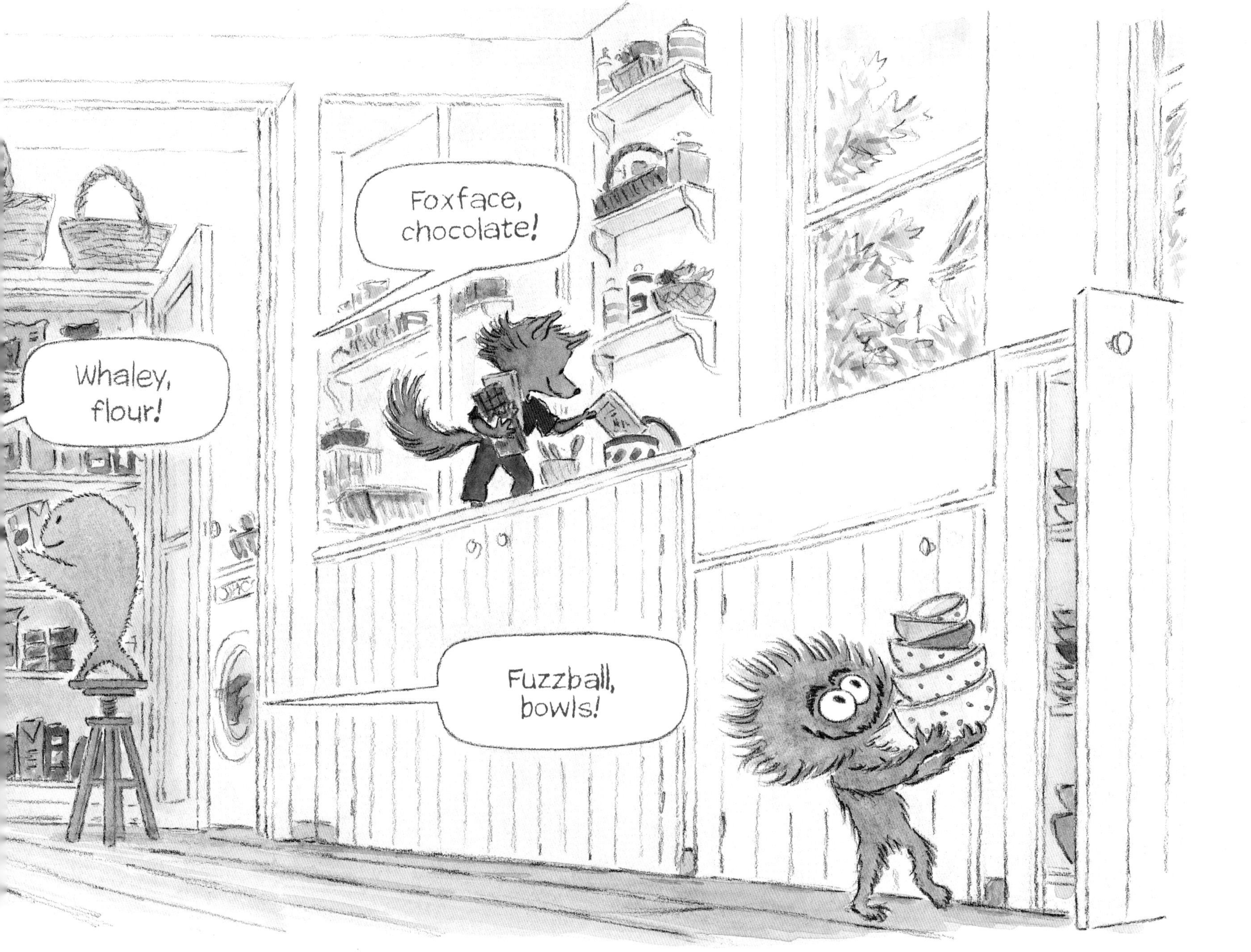
Whaley, flour!
Foxface, chocolate!
Fuzzball, bowls!

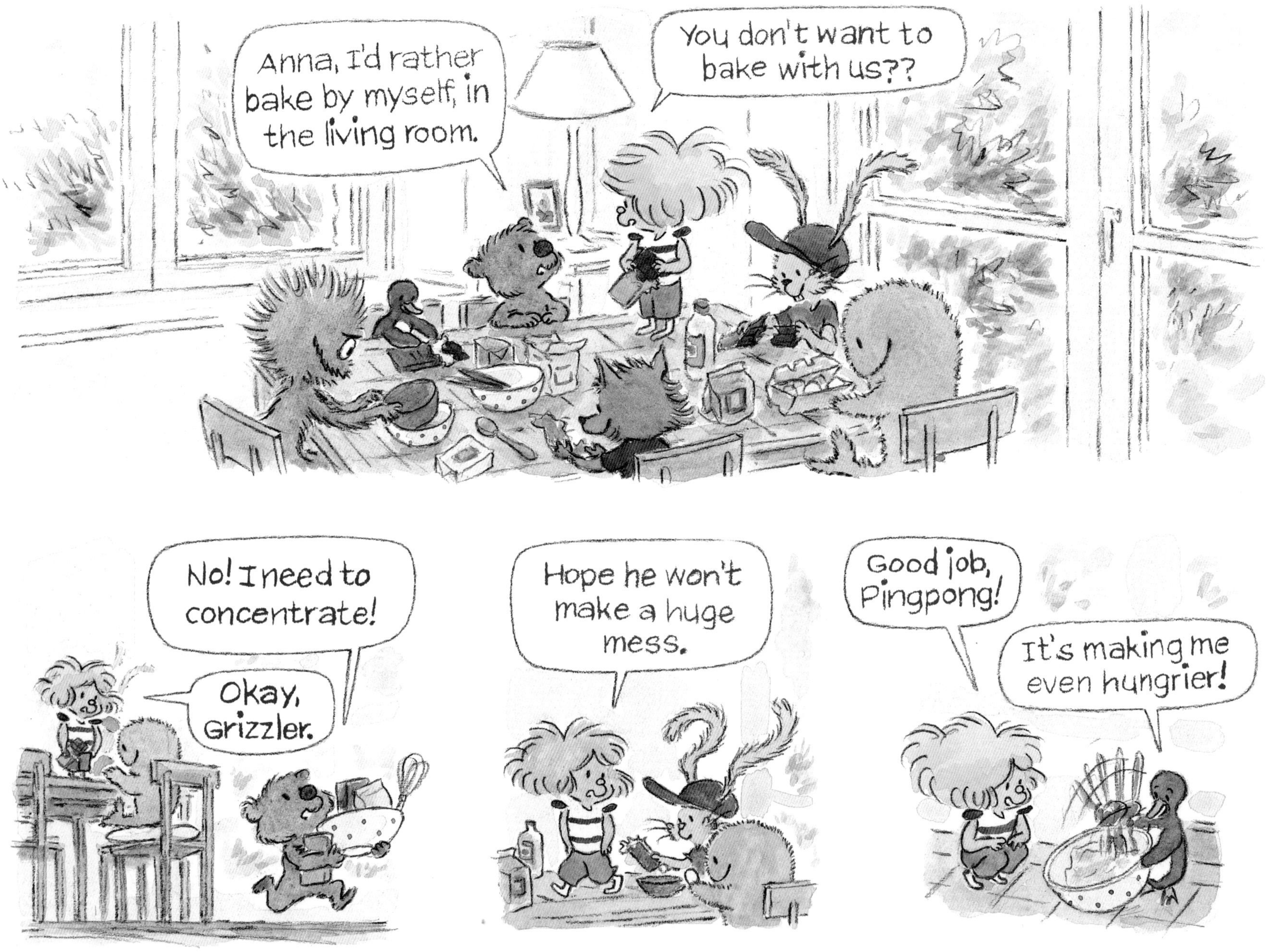
Anna, I'd rather bake by myself, in the living room.
You don't want to bake with us??
No! I need to concentrate!
Okay, Grizzler.
Hope he won't make a huge mess.
Good job, Pingpong!
It's making me even hungrier!

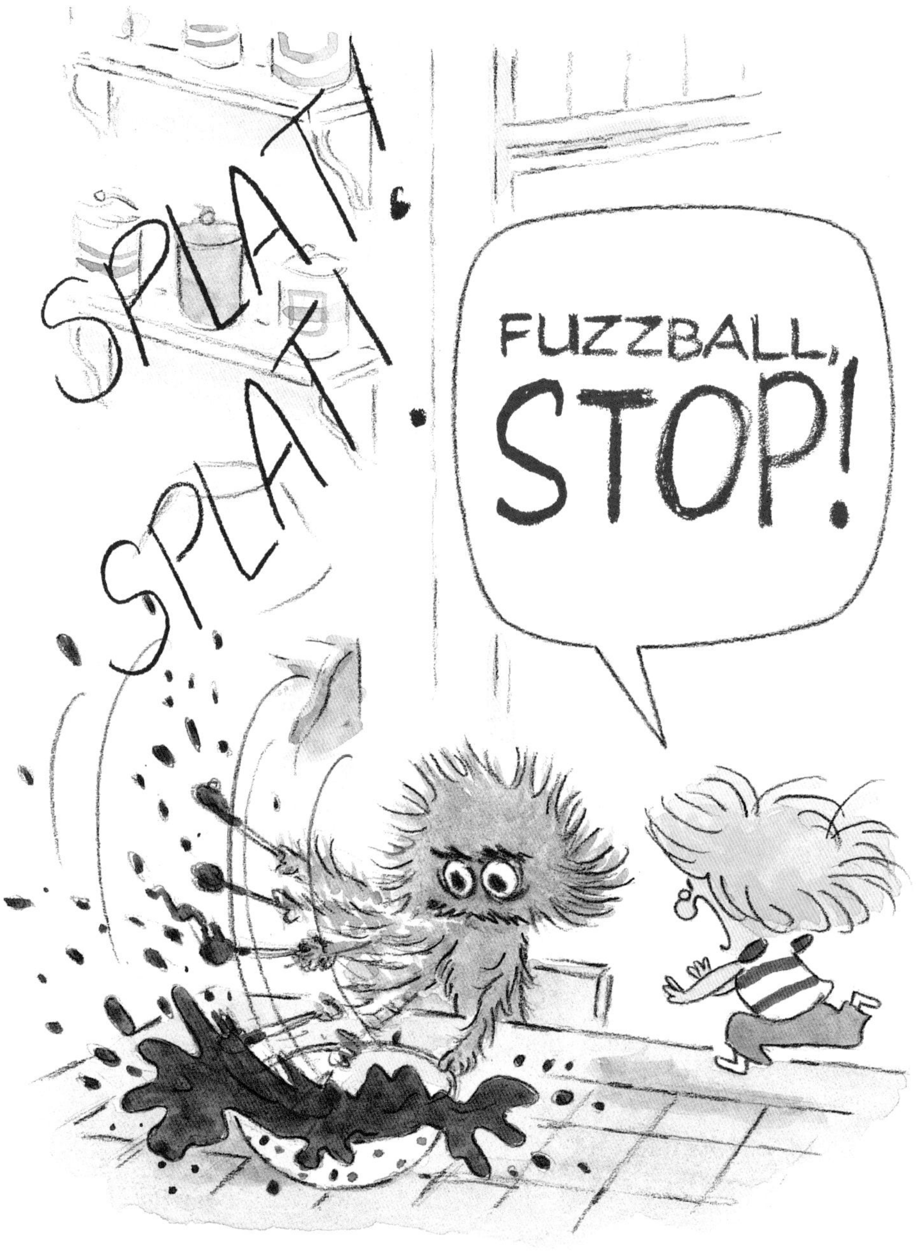
SPLAT!
SPLAT!
FUZZBALL,
STOP!

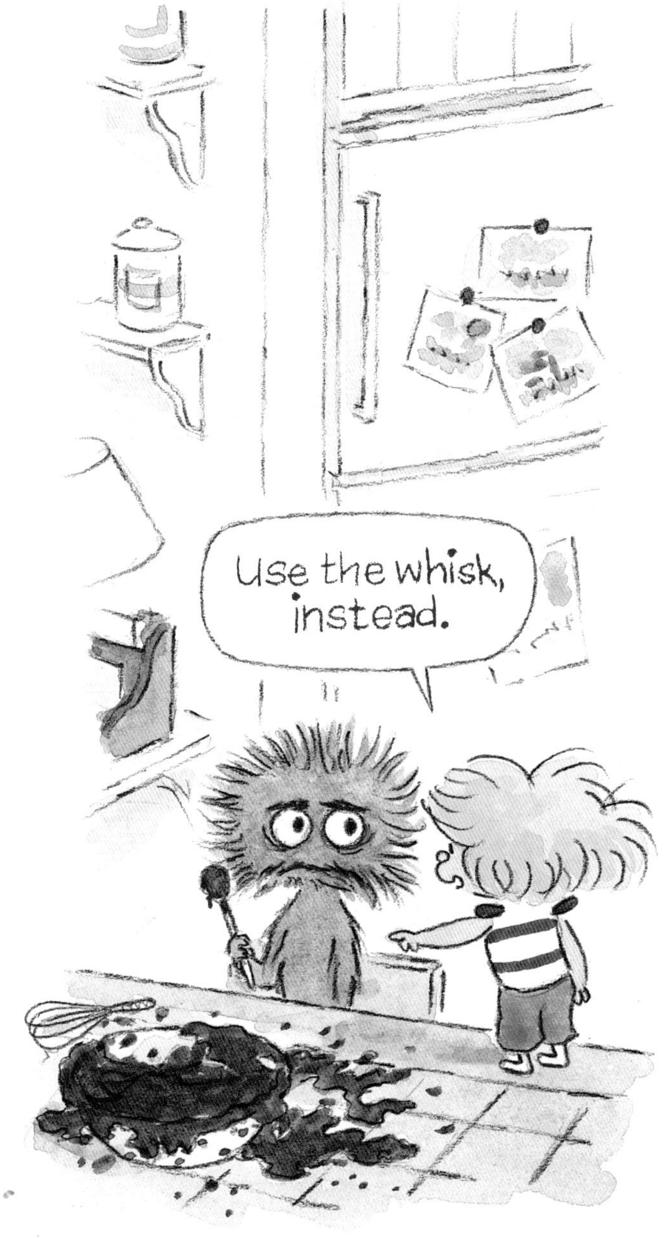
Use the whisk,
instead.

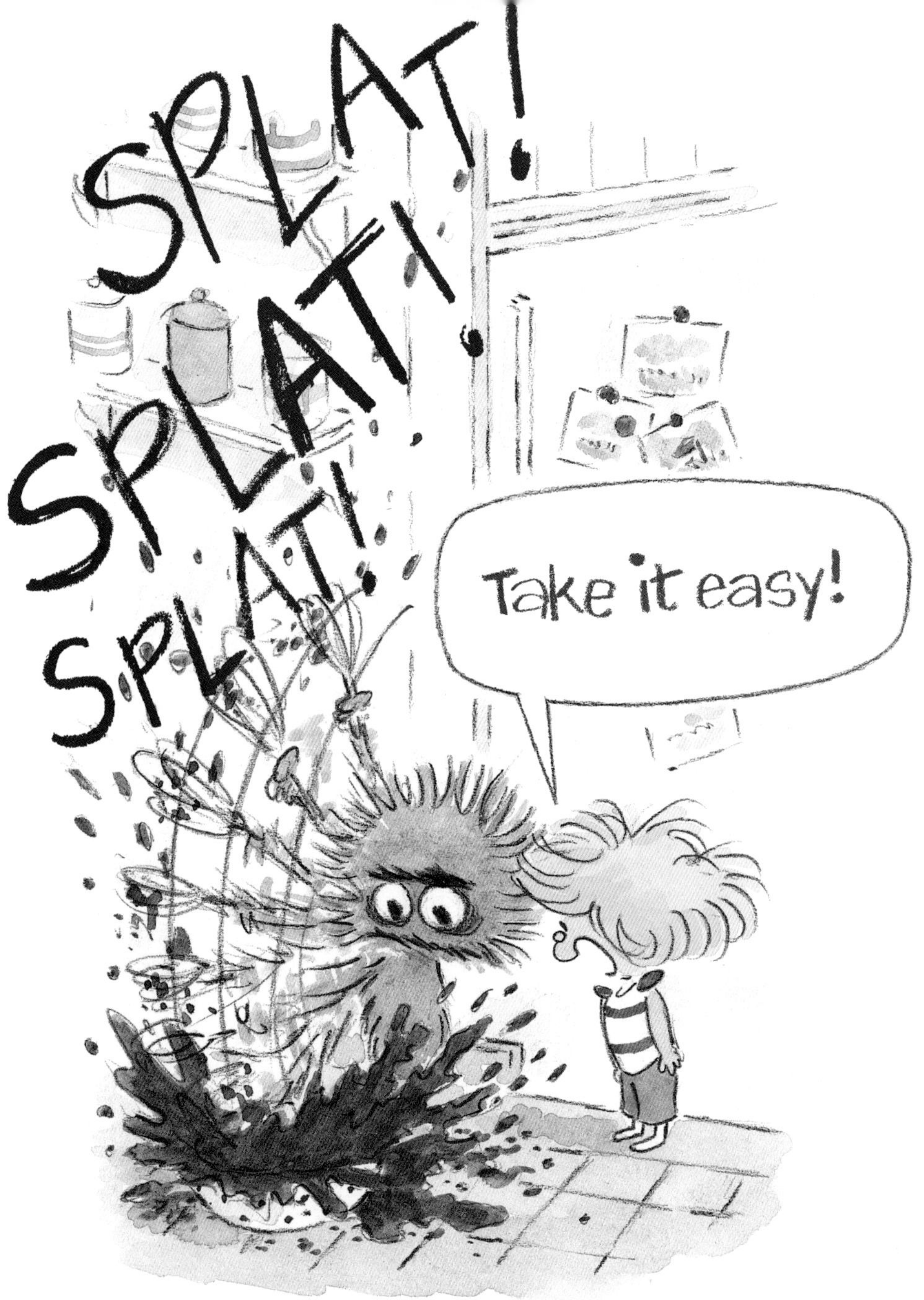
SPLAT!
SPLAT!
SPLAT!
Take it easy!

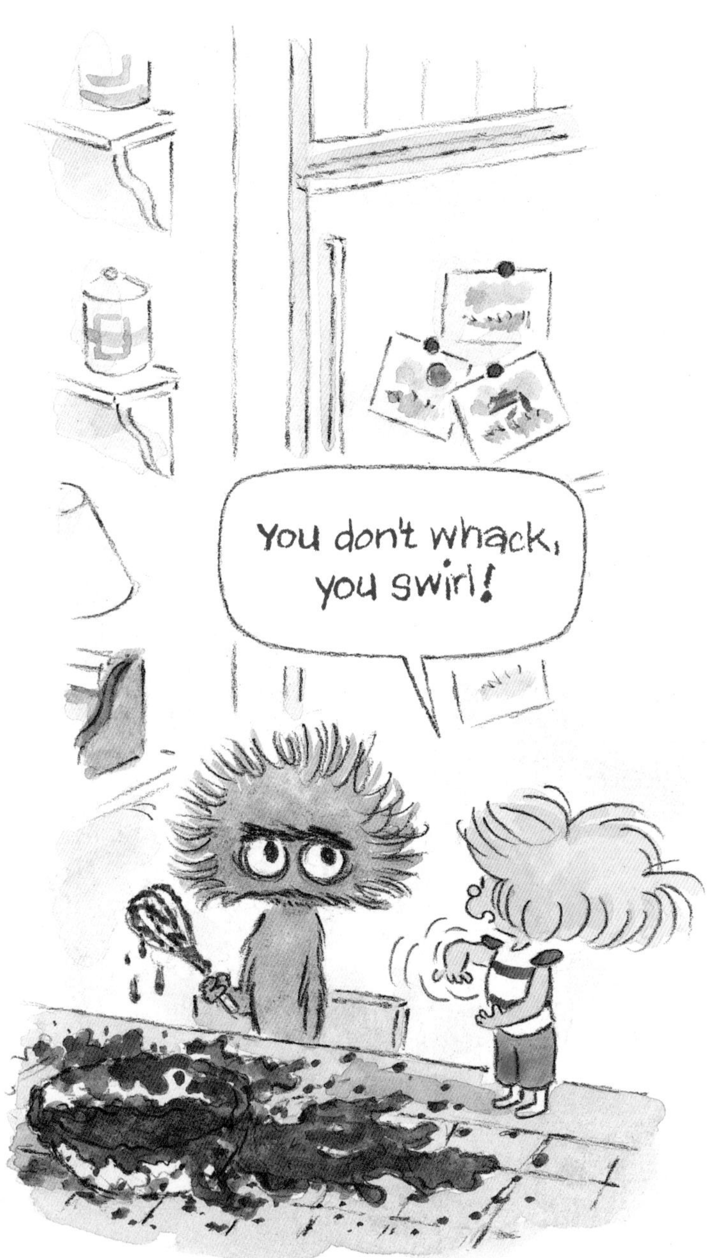
You don't whack, you swirl!

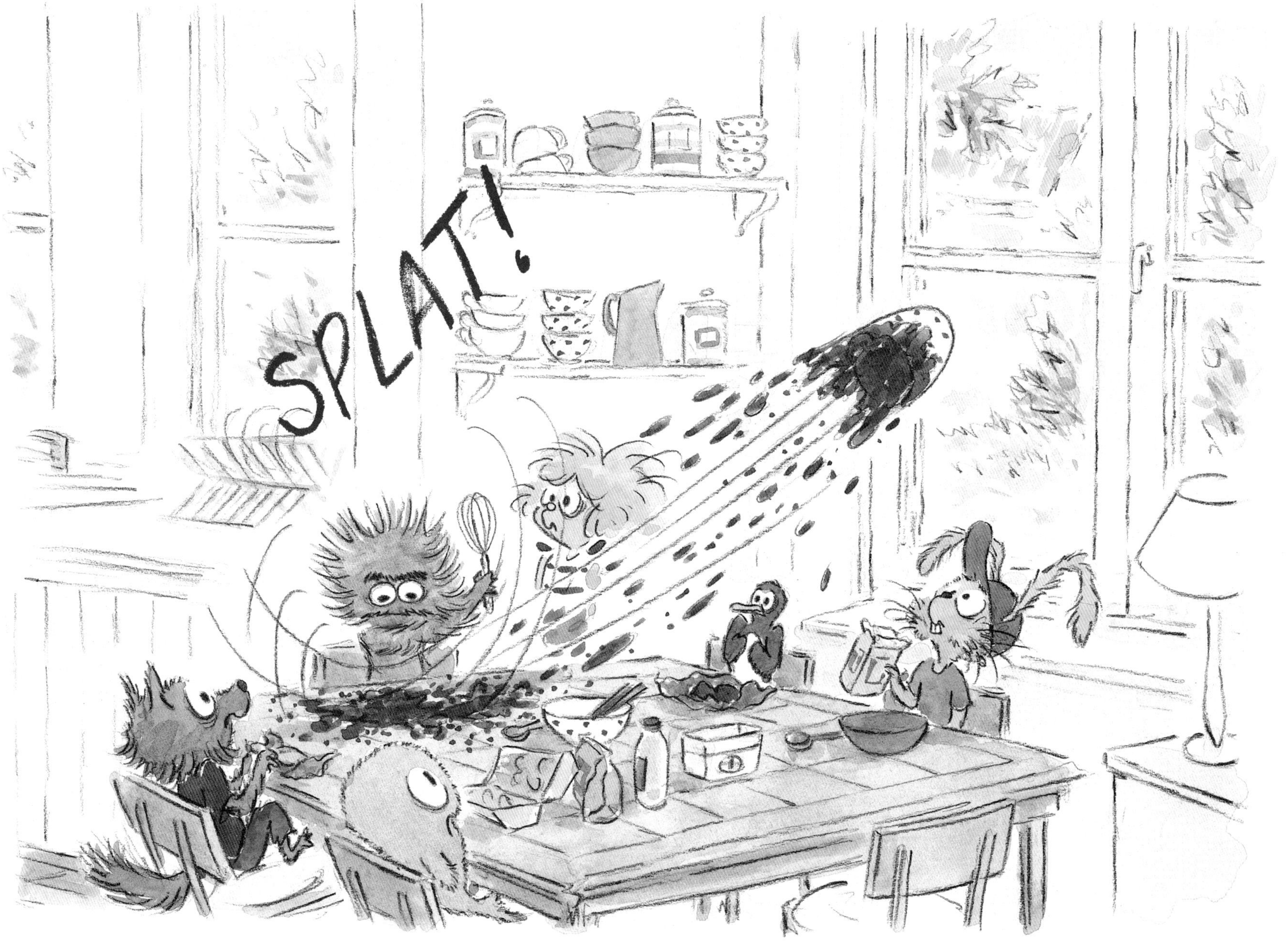
SPLAT!

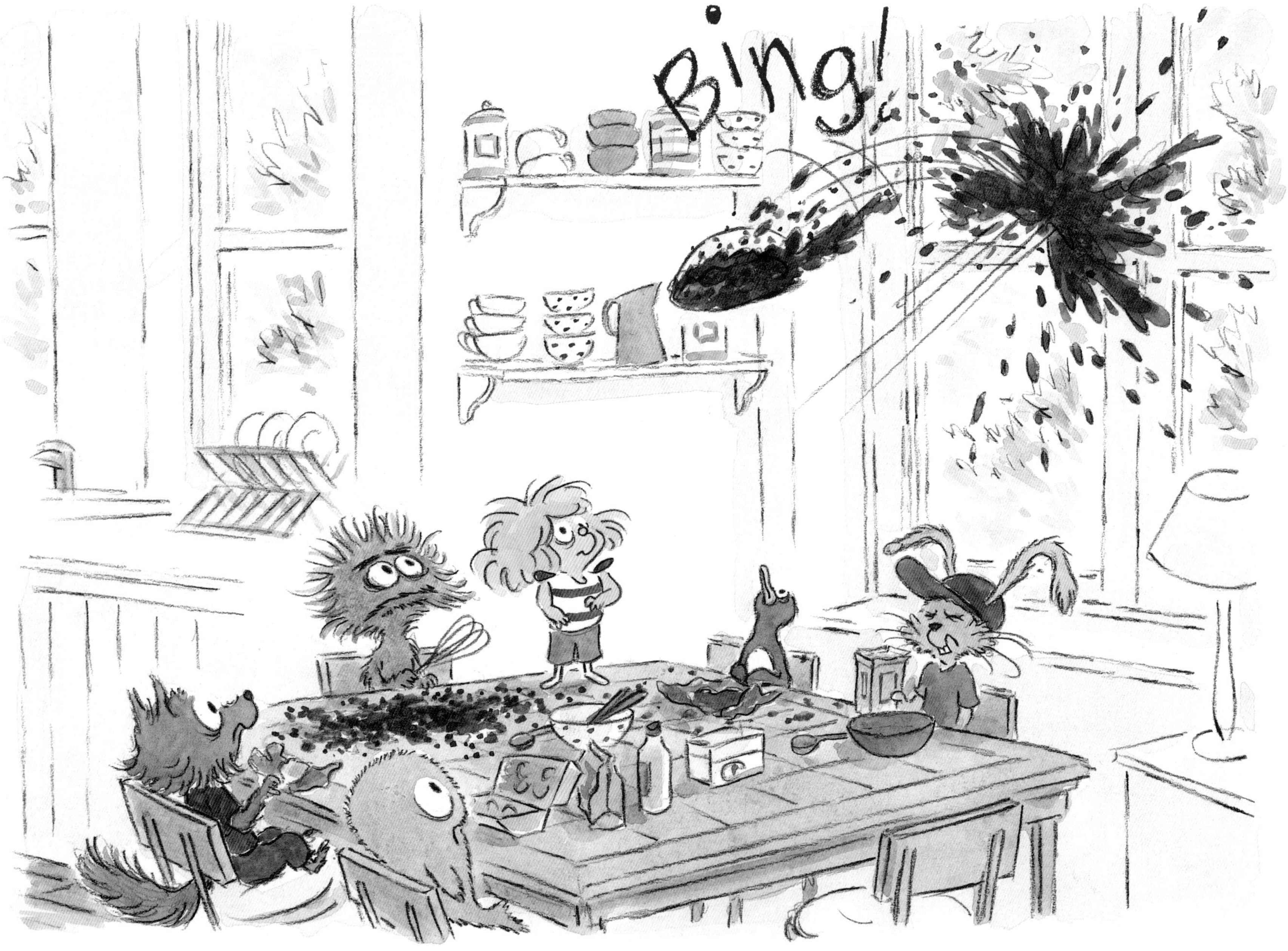
Bing!

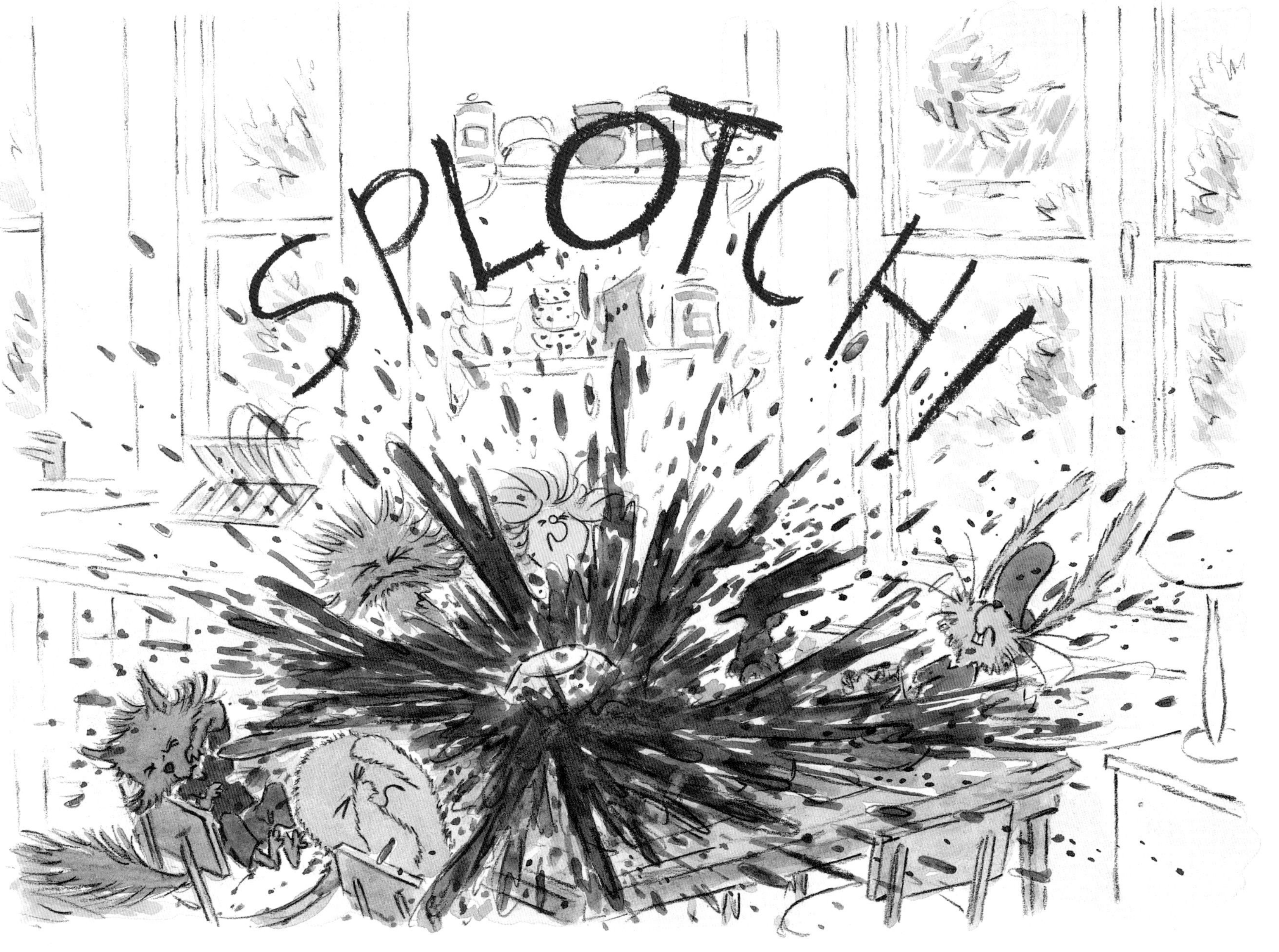
SPLOTCH!

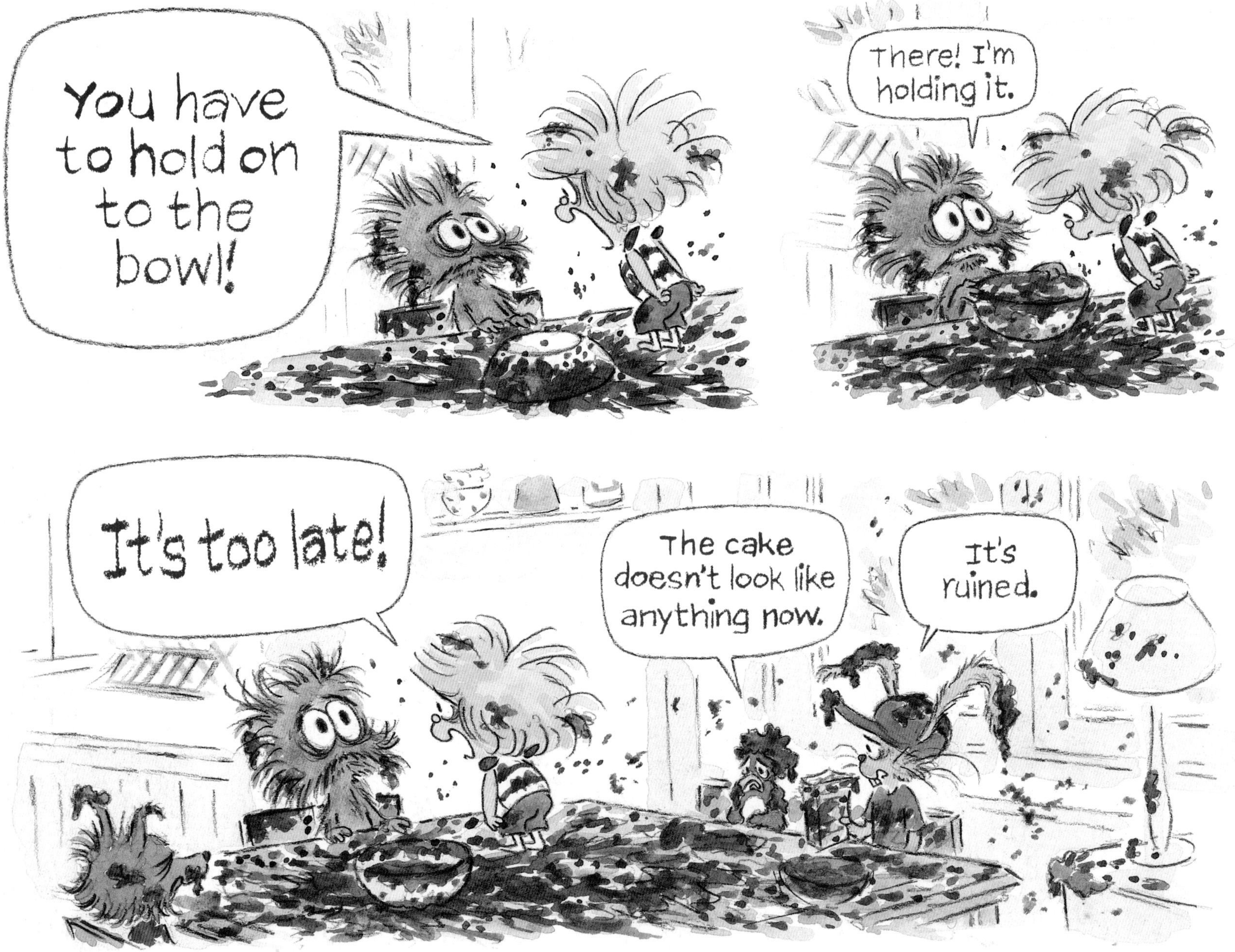
You have to hold on to the bowl!
There! I'm holding it.
It's too late!
The cake doesn't look like anything now.
It's ruined.

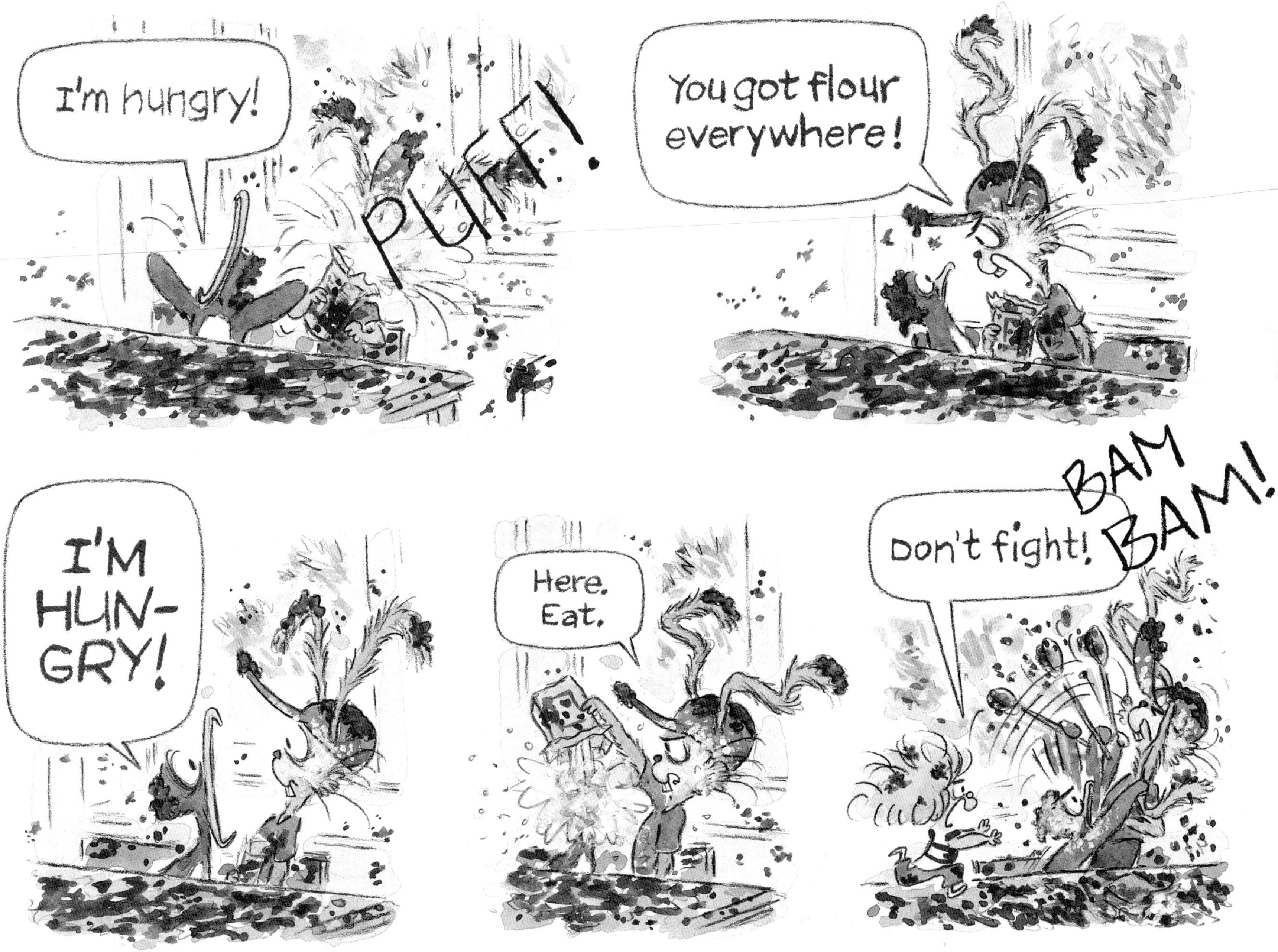

I'm hungry!
PUFF!
You got flour everywhere!
I'M HUN-GRY!
Here. Eat.
Don't fight!
BAM BAM!

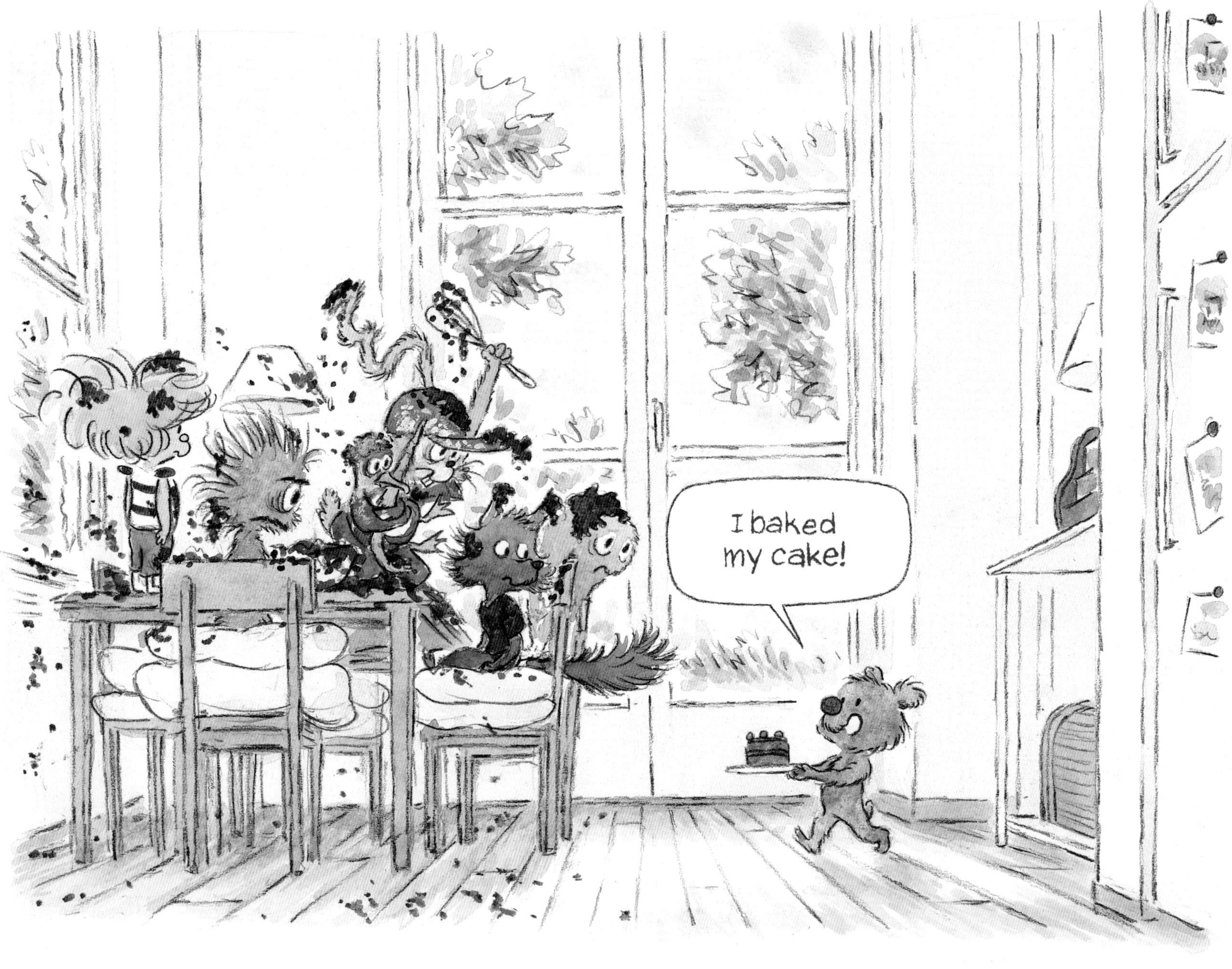
I baked my cake!

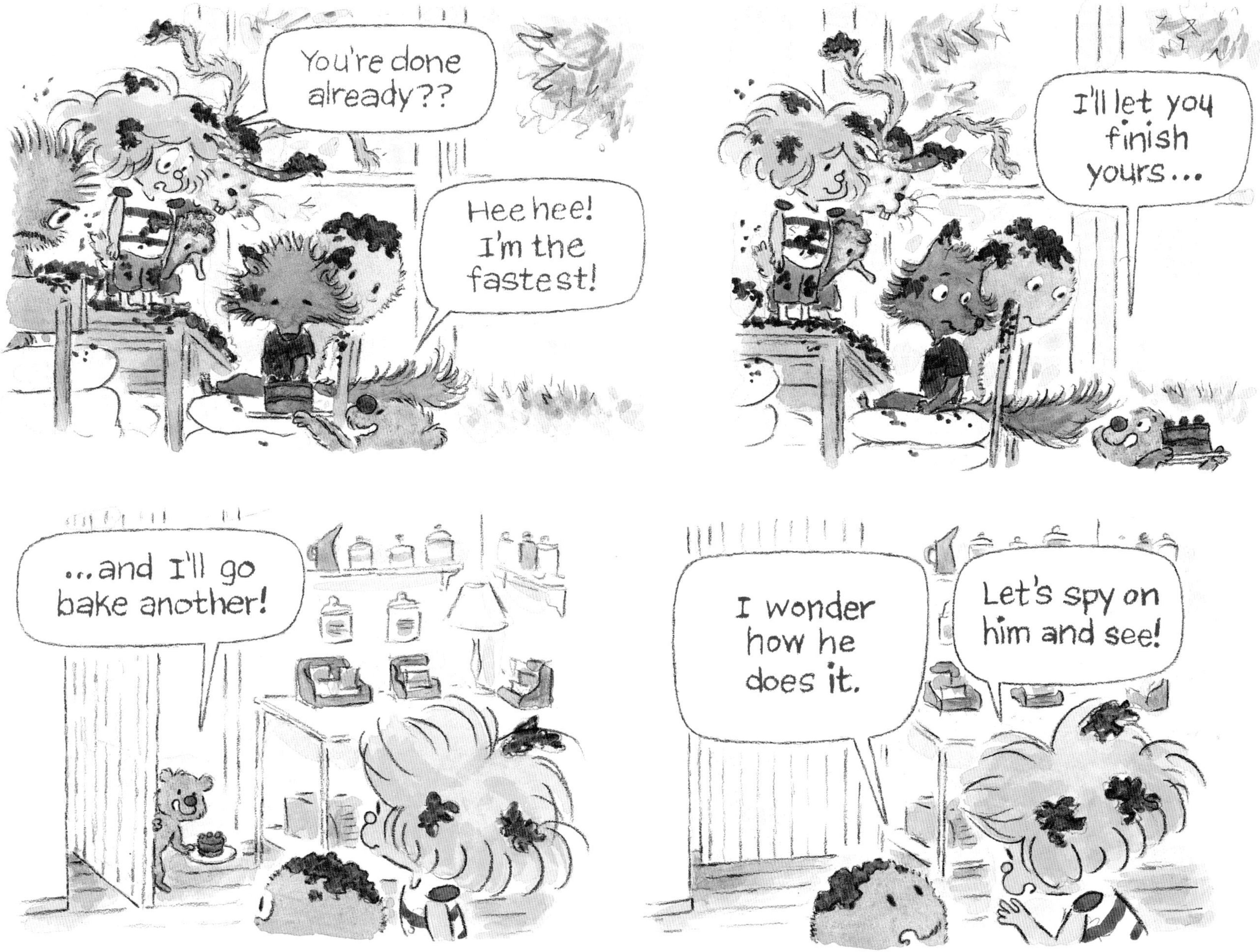
You're done already??
Hee hee! I'm the fastest!
I'll let you finish yours...
...and I'll go bake another!
I wonder how he does it.
Let's spy on him and see!

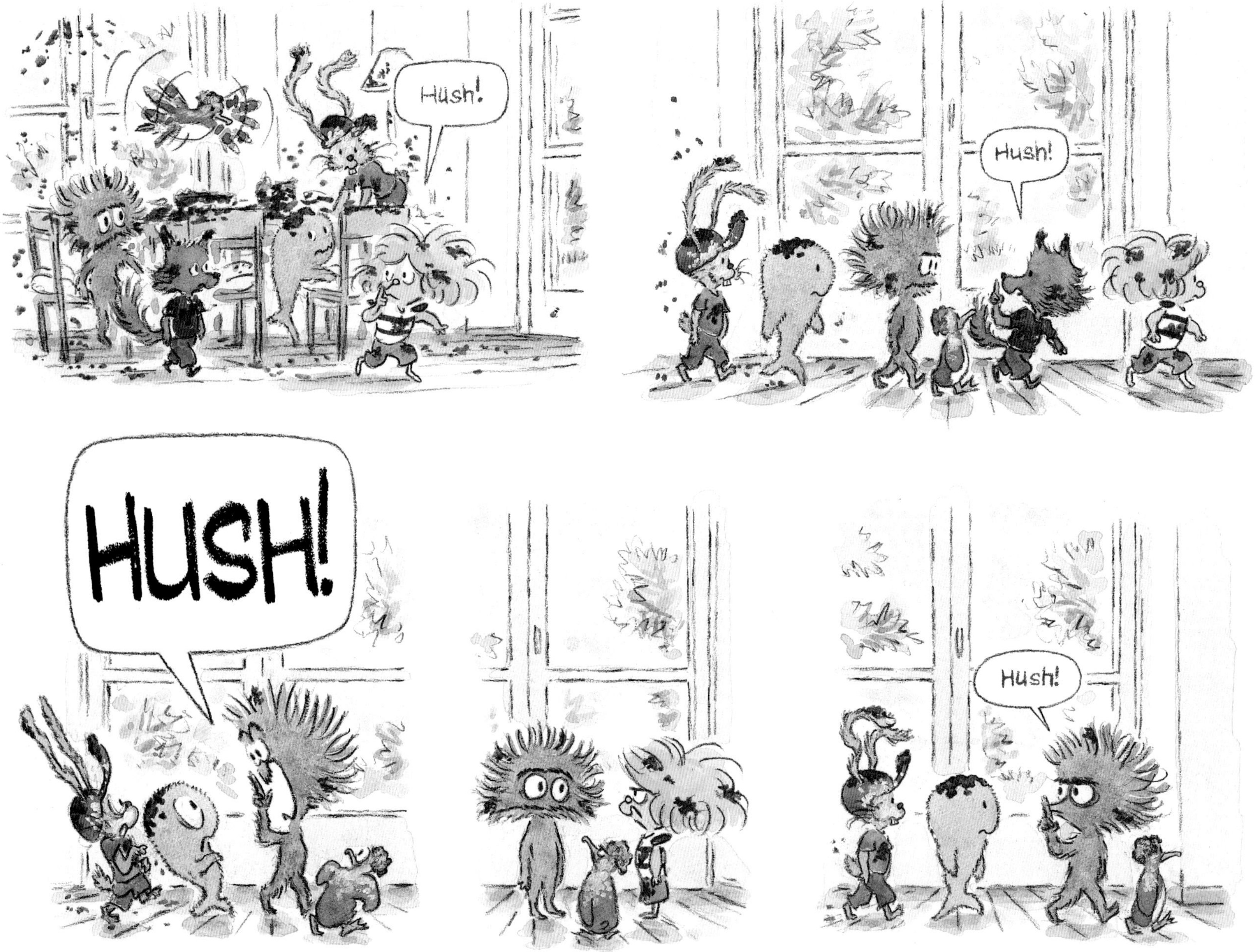
Hush!
Hush!
HUSH!
Hush!

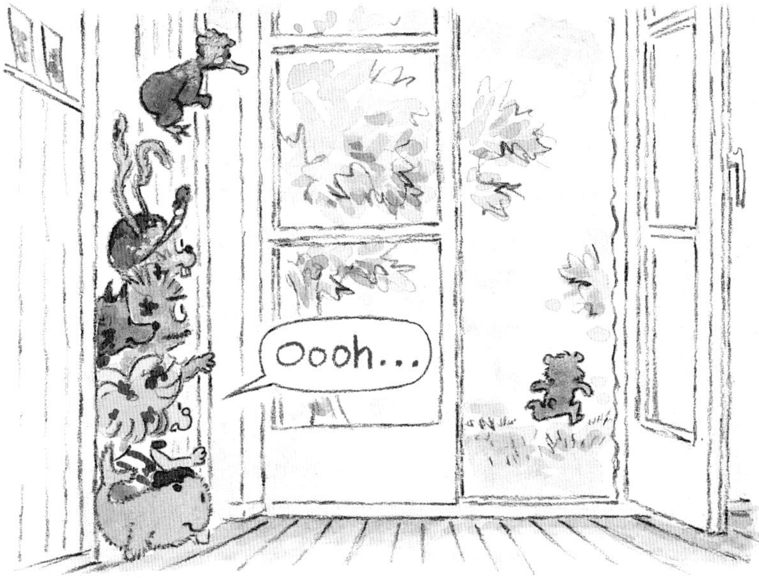
Oooh...

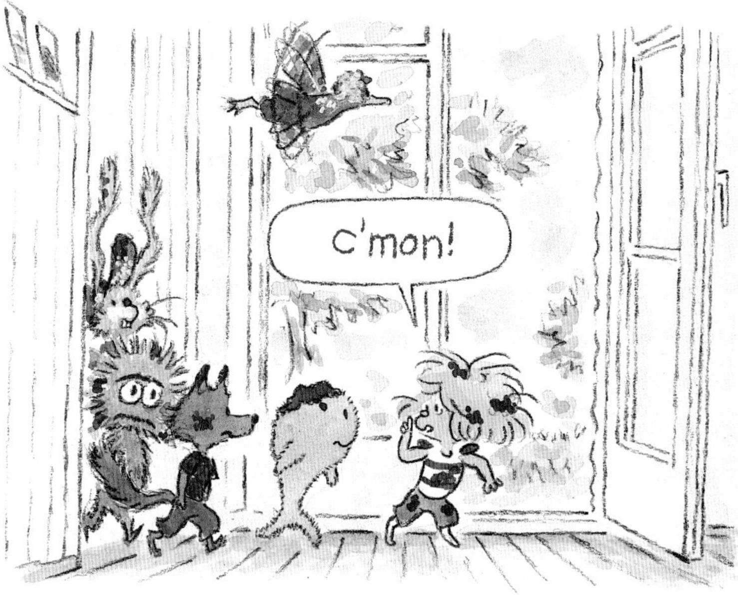
C'mon!

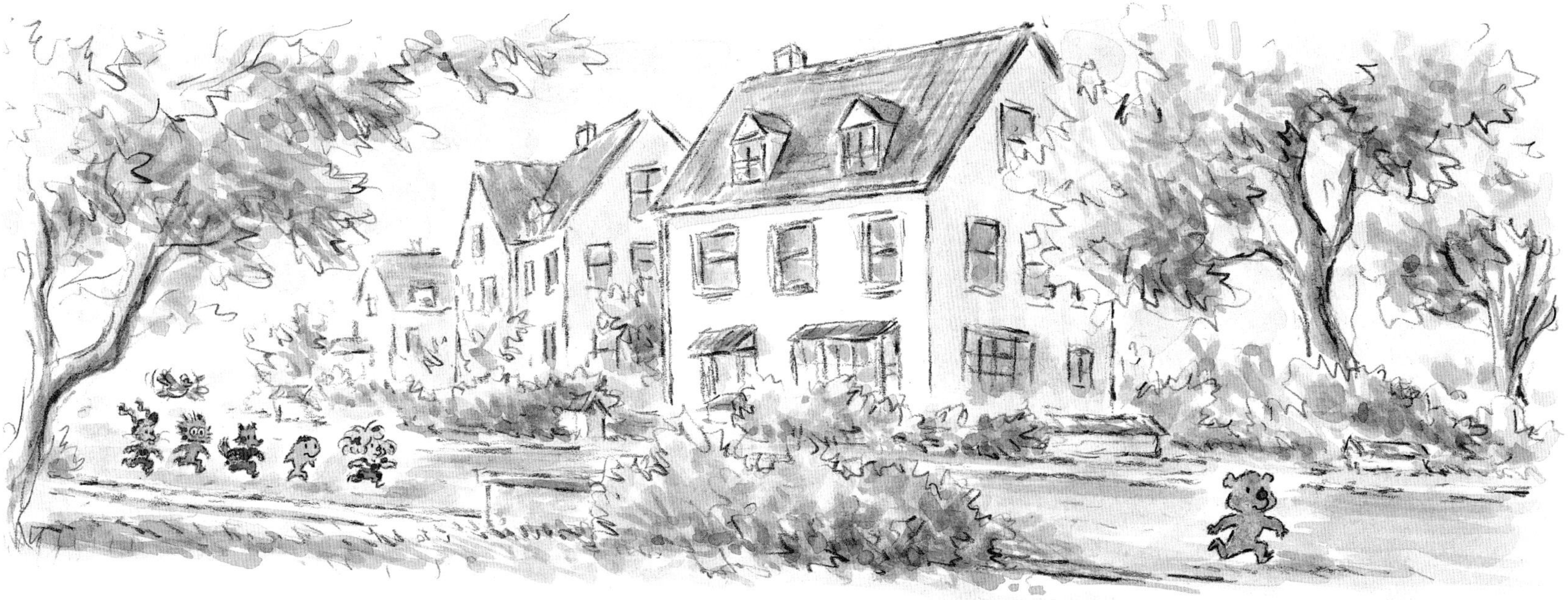

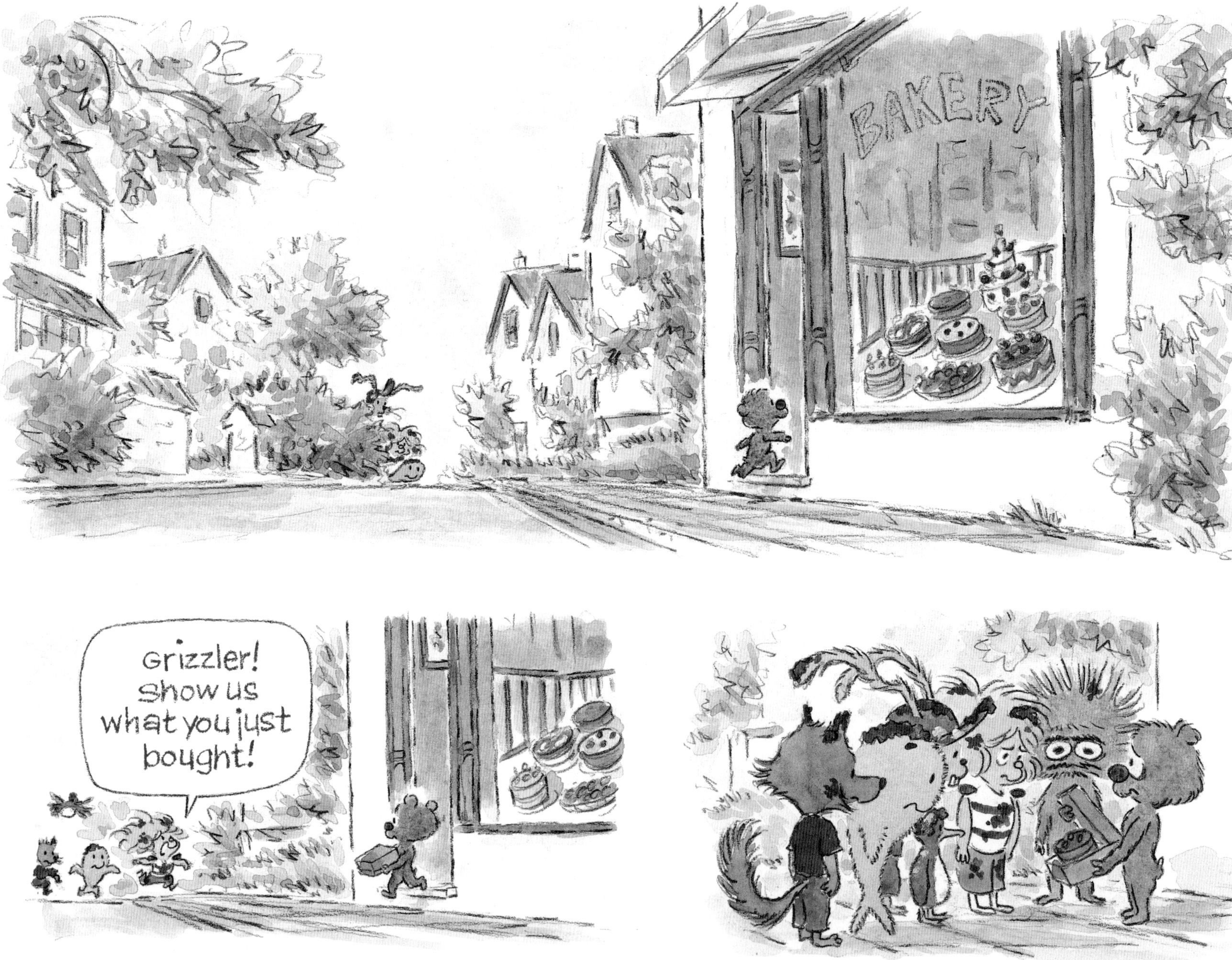
BAKERY
Grizzler! show us what you just bought!

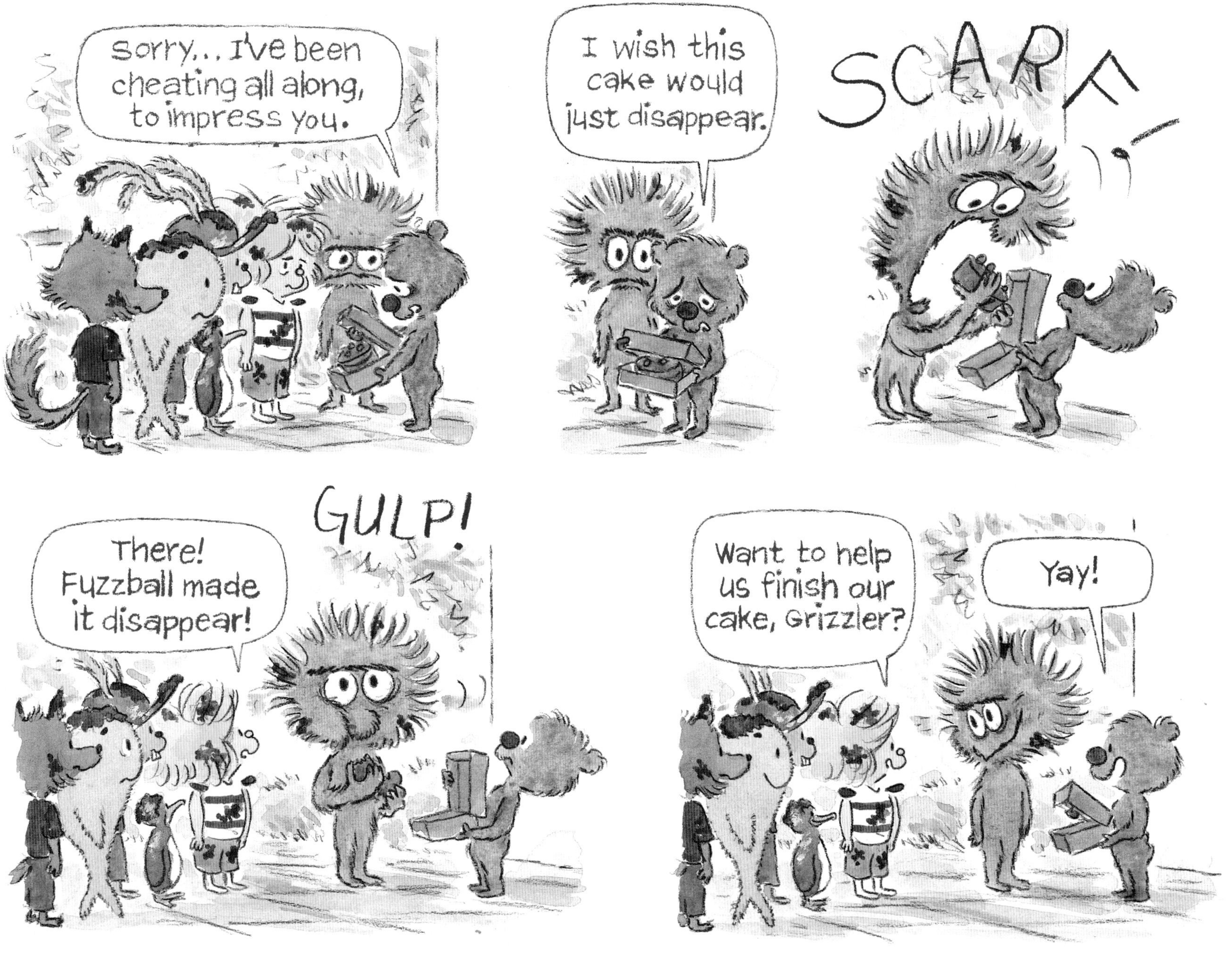
Sorry... I've been cheating all along, to impress you.
I wish this cake would just disappear.
SCARF
There! Fuzzball made it disappear!
GULP!
Want to help us finish our cake, Grizzler?
Yay!

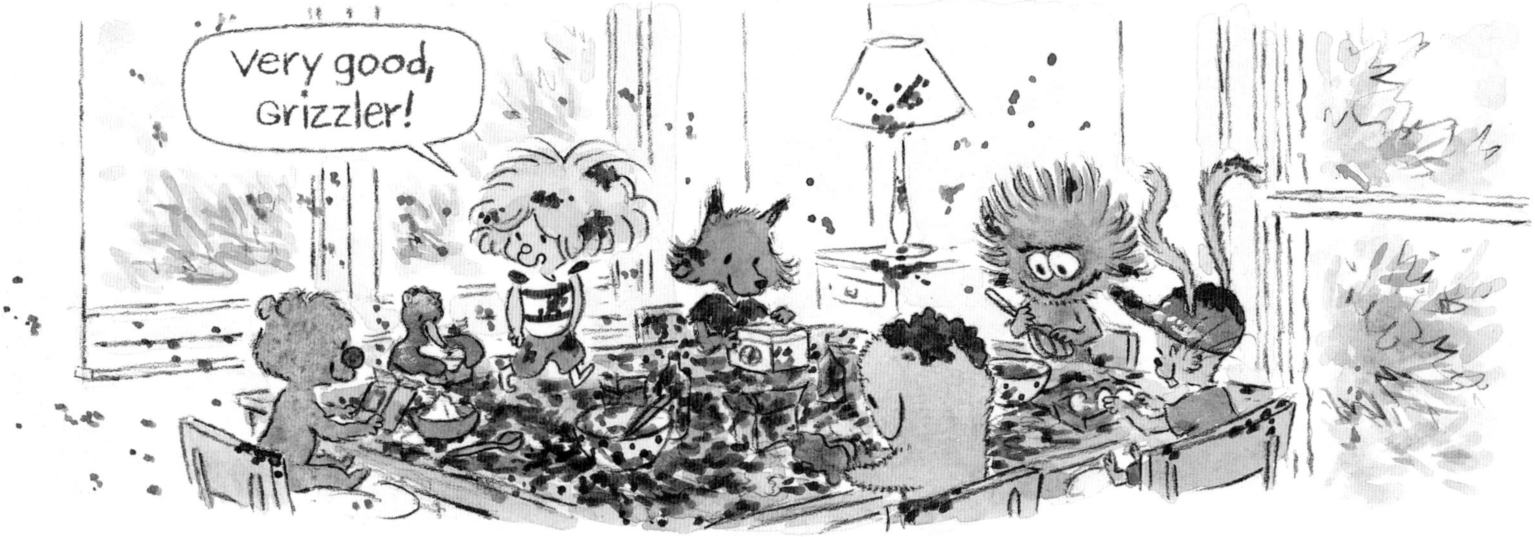
Very good, Grizzler!

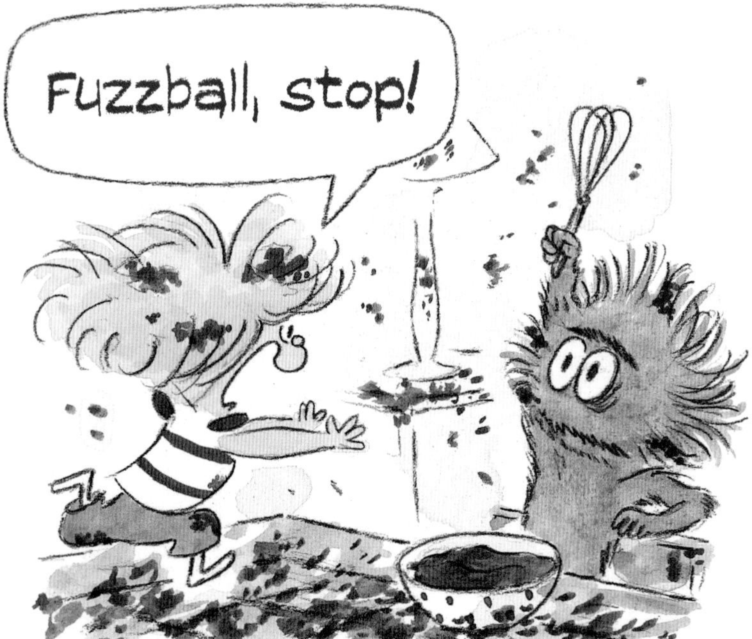
Fuzzball, stop!

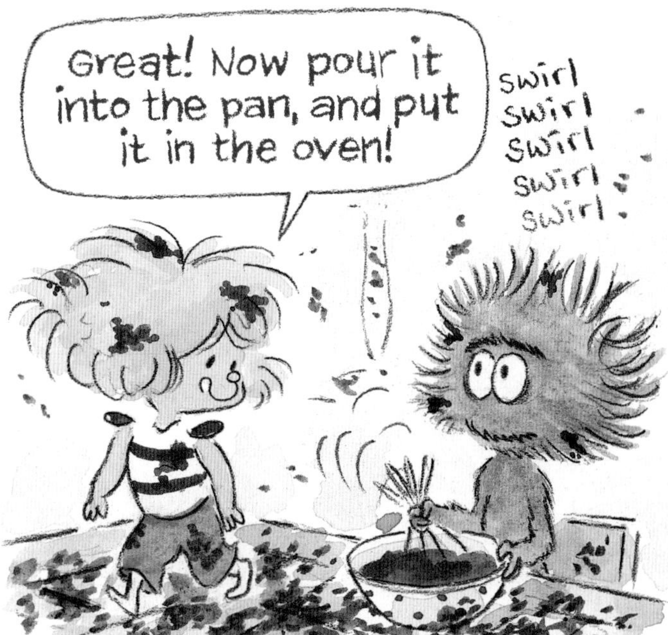
Great! Now pour it into the pan, and put it in the oven!
swirl
swirl
swirl
swirl
swirl

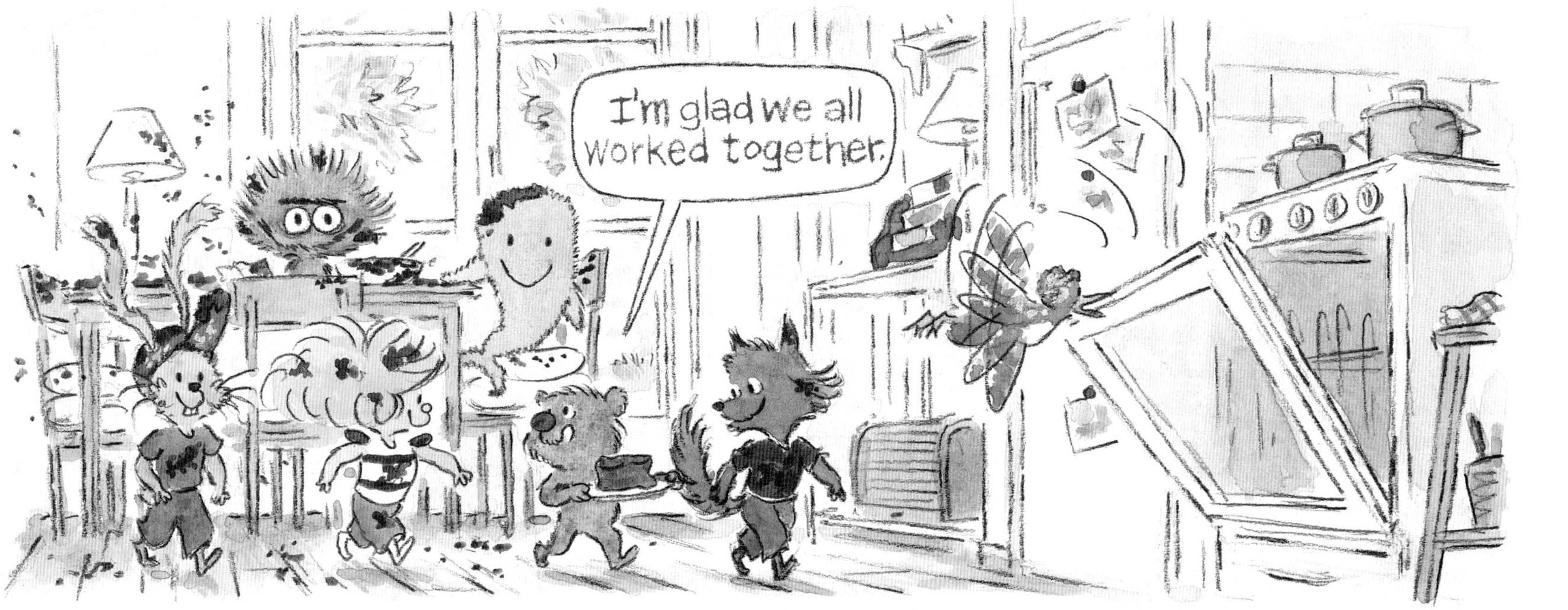
I'm glad we all worked together.

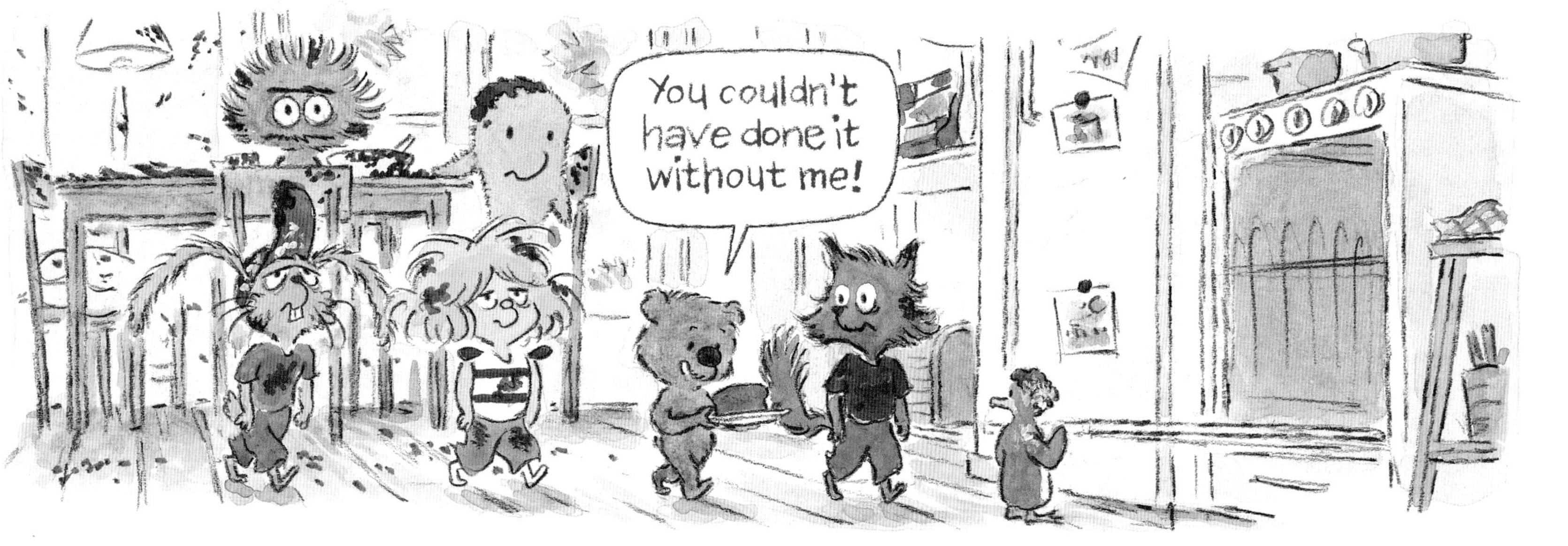
You couldn't have done it without me!

Bon appétit!

**First Second**

*Ana Ana - Déluge de chocolat* © Dargaud 2012 by Alexis Dormal & Dominique Roques
All rights reserved – www.dargaud.com

Lettering by Marion Vitus
English translation by Mark Siegel
English translation copyright © 2015 by First Second

Published by First Second
First Second is an imprint of Roaring Brook Press, a division of Holtzbrinck Publishing Holdings Limited Partnership
175 Fifth Avenue, New York, New York 10010
All rights reserved

Cataloging-in-Publication Data is on file at the Library of Congress

ISBN: 978-1-62672-020-6

First Second books may be purchased for business or promotional use. For information on bulk purchases please contact
Macmillan Corporate and Premium Sales Department at (800) 221-7945 x5442 or by email at
specialmarkets@macmillan.com.

Originally published in French as *Ana Ana: Déluge de chocolat*.
First American edition 2015
Book design by Colleen AF Venable

Printed in China by South China Printing Co. Ltd., Dongguan City, Guangdong Province

10 9 8 7 6 5 4 3 2 1